D0994616

This book belongs to

This edition published by Parragon in 2011

Parragon
Queen Street House
4 Queen Street
Bath BA1 1HE, UK

Copyright © Parragon Books Ltd 2009

All rights reserved. No part of this publication may be reproduced,
stored in a retrieval system or transmitted, in any form or by
any means, electronic, mechanical, photocopying, recording or
otherwise, without the prior permission of the copyright holder.

ISBN 978-1-4454-5420-7

Printed in China

thank you
for being my friend

Peter Bently   Gill McLean

Bath · New York · Singapore · Hong Kong · Cologne · Delhi
Melbourne · Amsterdam · Johannesburg · Auckland · Shenzhen

It was a dark night. In the bedroom, nothing stirred.

Nothing except a heap of bright wrapping paper on the end of the bed.

The paper rustled.

It crackled.

It shook.

And then out popped a toy horse.

"Hello!" said the horse. "I'm Cleo."

But there was no answer.

Cleo trotted across the bed. "Where is everybody?" she wondered, "I don't like the dark and…

Oof!"

Cleo tumbled

onto the floor.

There were strange shapes in the dark.
"I'm scared," shivered Cleo.

"I can see monsters!"

There was a thin monster…
a plump monster…
a tall monster…
and a monster with no head!

Cleo saw a faint gleam.
A light!
Trying not to wake any
of the monsters, she
tiptoed carefully
towards the door.

She **tumbled** out onto the landing.

"Oh," said Cleo,
"it's only the moon." Suddenly
a cloud slid over the moon and
everything went dark.

And then something downstairs went

BONG!

BONG!

Cleo nearly jumped out of her skin.
"Another monster!" she whinnied.

BONG!

BONG!

"Help!"
neighed Cleo.

Cleo spun on her hooves
and galloped back the way
she had come.

Cleo hurtled into the bedroom and
tripped over something on the floor.

"Ugh," groaned the Thing drowsily.
"Who... who are you?"

"I'm C-Cleo," stuttered Cleo.
"P-please don't gobble me up!"

Then the moon came out again and Cleo saw
that the Thing was a fluffy yellow duck.
"I'm Daphne," smiled the duck. "And why
would I want to gobble you up?"

Cleo told Daphne all about the monsters.

"The monsters won't get you," said Daphne.

"Promise?" asked Cleo with a big yawn.

"Promise," said Daphne kindly. "Why don't you snuggle down with me?"

"You won't go, will you?" said Cleo.

"No. You're safe now. Night-night," said Daphne.

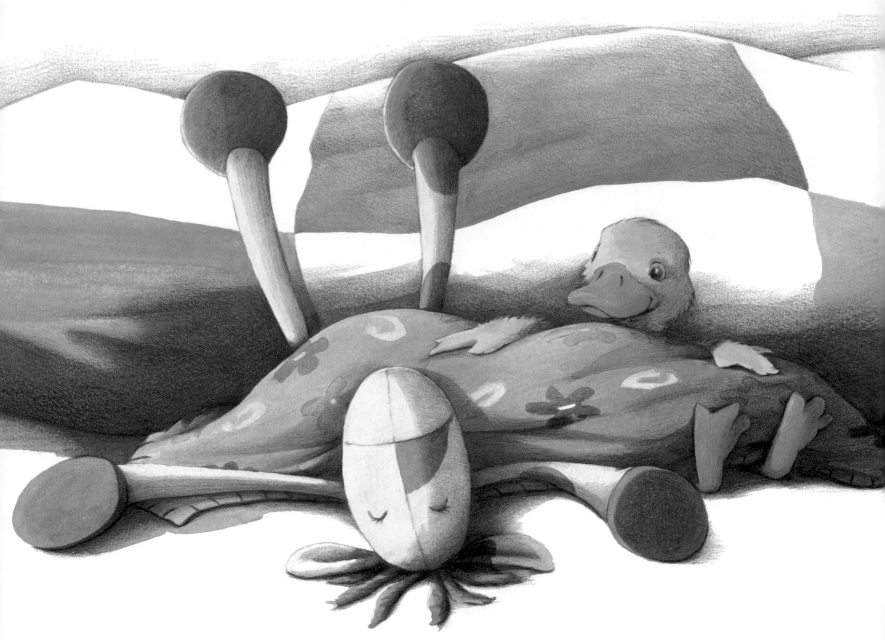

The next morning, Cleo peeped out
from under Daphne's wing.
She blinked in the bright sunlight.
"Morning, sleepyhead,"
quacked Daphne.
"Come and meet all the monsters!"

Cleo shot back under Daphne's wing.
"Don't worry," laughed Daphne.
"They won't eat you.
I promised, remember."

The thin monster was...

a lamp!

The plump monster was...

a heap of cushions!

The tall monster was... a wardrobe!

And the headless monster was...

a dressing gown!

And the one that chased Cleo was. . .

The
grandfather
clock!

Tick
Tock
Tick
Tock

"I've been really silly," smiled Cleo.
"No, you've not," said Daphne.
"Lots of things look scarier in the dark."

"I don't think I'll be scared any more," said Cleo. "Now that you're my friend."

The end